My Name

For _____ —S.K.
insert your name here

Dedicated to my fellow oddballs, misfits, and

wonderful weirdos —S.P.

Farrar Straus Giroux Books for Young Readers
An imprint of Macmillan Publishing Group, LLC
120 Broadway, New York, NY 10271 • mackids.com

Text copyright © 2023 by Supriya Kelkar
Pictures copyright © 2023 by Sandhya Prabhat

Our books may be purchased in bulk for promotional, educational, or business use.
Please contact your local bookseller or the Macmillan Corporate and Premium Sales Department
at (800) 221-7945 ext. 5442 or by email at MacmillanSpecialMarkets@macmillan.com.

Library of Congress Cataloging-in-Publication Data is available.

First edition, 2023
Color separations by Embassy Graphics
Printed in China by Hung Hing Off-set Printing Co. Ltd., Heshan City, Guangdong Province

ISBN 978-0-374-31463-7
1 3 5 7 9 10 8 6 4 2

The art for this book was created digitally using Adobe Photoshop. The text was set in Archer,
and the display type was created by Sandhya Prabhat. Designed and art directed by Aram Kim.
Production was supervised by John Nora, and the production editor was Allyson Floridia.
Edited by Grace Kendall, with support from Asia Harden.

My Name

WORDS BY
Supriya Kelkar

PICTURES BY
Sandhya Prabhat

Farrar Straus Giroux

New York

There will be so many new names on the first day.

Honor them and yours
the very same way.

Listen.
Connect.
Remember.
Reflect.

Say your new friends' names out loud
And the name belonging to you
Carefully, kindly
And they will too.

My name means giggles
And more names
That sound similar
But are not mine.

My name means spices
And far-off smells
Unseen colors
And sounds unheard to them.

My name means the hot sun
And sweaty crowds
When all I feel
Are frosty stares.

means

syllable

After syllable

Rolling,

crashing,

unending

Like the waves in the sea.

My name means

I'M DIFFERENT.

Your name means
you're you.

Your name means wrinkled faces
Creased into smiles
Unknotted hearts
And lips twisted with love to welcome you.

Your name means giggles
Happy giggles
And many more names
All belonging to you.

Teammate!

Your name means spices
And spiraling, scented steam
Clanging dishes and
A rainbow on your plate.

Your name means warmth
Like the first summer breeze
Wrapping us together
With those who came before.

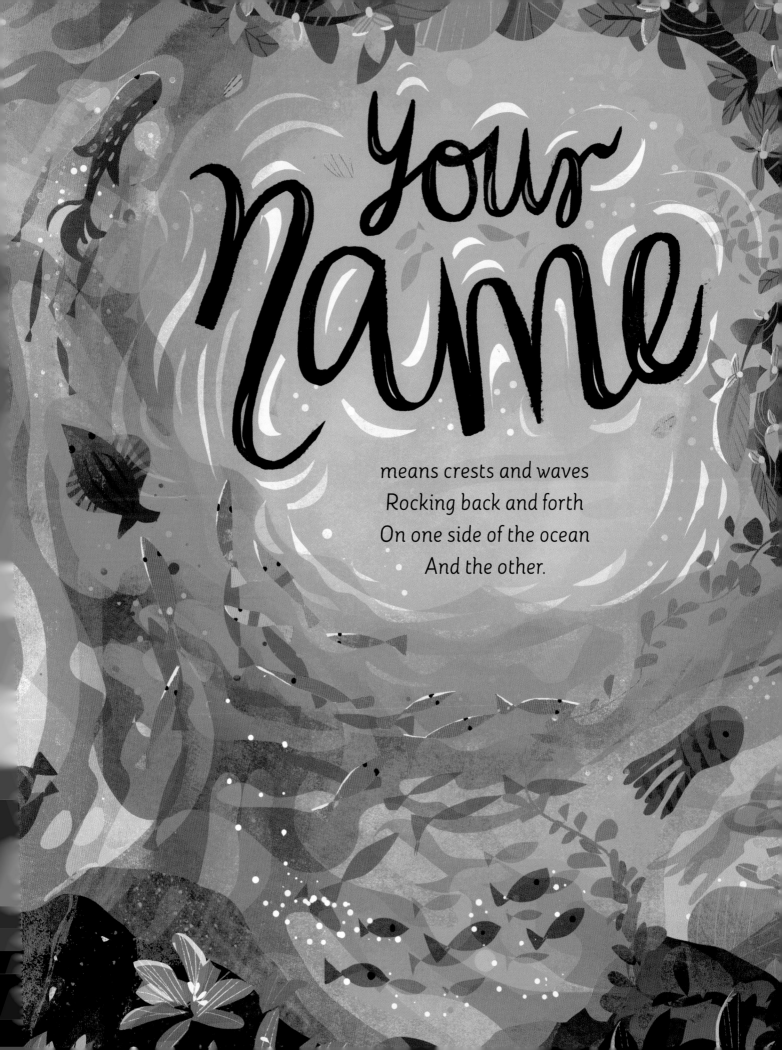

Your Name

means crests and waves
Rocking back and forth
On one side of the ocean
And the other.

Your name means you're different.
Your name means you're you.

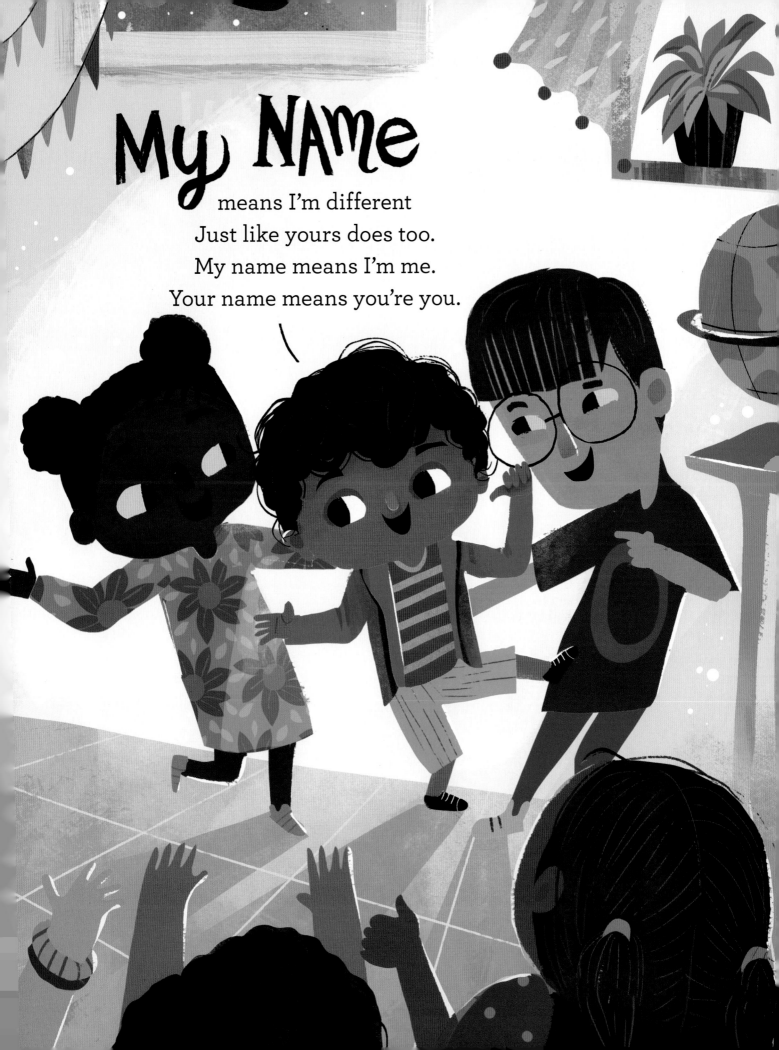

My Name

means I'm different
Just like yours does too.
My name means I'm me.
Your name means you're you.

AUTHOR'S NOTE

My name is Supriya.

"Supriya" means "beloved by all." My dad picked the name out because that's what I was, my parents' beloved child. (I try to remind my younger brother of this often.)

But despite the beauty and power in that name, do you know what nickname my friends started calling me when I was in elementary school?

Soup.

And I went with it. I even liked it. It was fun and silly and went with my personality better than that long, three-syllable Indian name no one else in school had. That name that tripped up strangers and people who had known me for years alike. "Soup" felt easier, for me and for others, even if it wasn't filled with my father's love.

So I embraced the nickname. I even signed notes to friends with a drawing of a little smiling bowl of steaming-hot soup from elementary school through high school.

Because pretending I shared a name with a food everyone was familiar with was easier than dealing with the embarrassment and shame I felt when people couldn't say my real name or purposely butchered it, or when they'd tell me how beautiful my name was after I had pronounced it for them. Because even though one of those sentiments is a positive, to me they all meant the same thing: *Your name means you're different.*

Whenever a teacher took a pause during attendance on the first day of school, I would apologetically admit the name that had stumped them was mine and say it for them, pronouncing it a little less like it was meant to be said, to make it easier for everyone. To be a little less different.

It took me years to realize our differences are to be celebrated, and many more years to like my name and realize how much it says about who I am. I no longer use that familiar nickname. I no longer apologetically say my name when someone mispronounces it or doesn't take the effort to even attempt saying it.

Instead, I hold my head up high, knowing that I do not need to apologize for my name or mispronounce it for someone else's convenience. I hope this book serves as a reminder to everyone to be proud of your own name and to take the time to learn and pronounce other people's names correctly too.

Because *your name means you're different.* And that's a good thing.

Your name means you're you.

SOUP

Supriya

ILLUSTRATOR'S NOTE

My name is Sandhya Prabhat. I am from India, and I live in the United States now. People who are not of Indian descent have a hard time pronouncing my first name. I've been called Sandra, Sania, and Sandy so often! When I received the script for this book, I related to it deeply and couldn't wait to illustrate it.

Supriya's rhythmic and lyrical storytelling involved mirroring and revisiting scenes from the first part (the boy feeling embarrassed or frustrated) in the second part (the boy embracing his name), and I tried to do the same with my illustrations. I used recurring but modified imagery: mirroring spreads one after another, and turning cold, uncomfortable scenes in blue and green into warm and friendly moments in shades of orange and brown and yellow as his perspective changed.

The inspiration for the cover came from a Maya Angelou quote that I love: "I come as one, but I stand as ten thousand." Although the boy stands alone, he isn't lonely. He brings with him his foremothers and forefathers, his friends and family, and feels strong and supported.

I illustrated this book while facing the challenges of the pandemic, while raising my baby, and while visiting my family in India for a few months after eons of being apart. This project was my breath of fresh air, my window of escape. Painting it was often the only activity that helped me find my inner peace. I'm forever grateful to have had a chance to be a part of this project.